The Ripple

Written by Monica Stoltzfus
Illustrated by Alexandra H. MacVean

Pat wakes up with a smile.
He dresses, eats breakfast and
rides down the elevator…with a smile.

He walks through the lobby and stops at Mr. Clyde.
Pat gives him a huge smile and a hearty, "Good Morning."
Mr. Clyde stayed grumpy.

Pat smiles anyway and walks down the street.

He holds the door for the lady with the big hat and muffles, "You look nice today"...

Who then lends her umbrella
to the crossing guard
as it starts to sprinkle…

Who begins bellowing a song to the school children passing safely through the intersection...

Who laugh and giggle, skipping into their classrooms,
meeting their teachers with cheery faces.

But throughout Pat's day, his smile and his cheer fade away.

"Why me?" he wonders. "What did I do wrong?"

He walks home with a grimace. He rides up the elevator with a frown. He eats his dinner with a pout and goes to sleep…gloomy and grumpy.

The next day,
Pat decides to
stay in bed.
All day.

That morning, old Mr. Clyde meets the tenants with a grumpy old scowl...

The lady with the big hat chases her hat down the street, and yells at the crossing guard…

Who muddles the school traffic, making everyone late…

And the children race into their classrooms,wild and worried,
as their teachers walk in.

There seem to be far fewer cheery faces today.

That night, Aunt Edna comes to see Pat. "I'm just a kid so small and so young," he sighs.

"What difference does it make if I stay in bed for just one day?

"You know, the smallest stone still makes a ripple in the water. You are more important than you think," she replies.

Together they look out at the big bustling city through the small apartment window.

"There are many people out there, it's true. But the one thing the world might be missing is YOU."

Pat peers out
the tiny window again.
He scans the city streets,
amazed at what
he sees.

He stops his gaze on a familiar face.
It's old Mr. Clyde's.
He looks back at Aunt Edna with wide eyes.

"Do I make a difference to Mr. Clyde?" he asks. She smiles back at him.

Pat thinks for a moment. "Maybe, just maybe," he decided.

So, the very next day…
Pat gets up with a smile.
He dresses, eats breakfast,
and rides down the elevator…with a smile.

He walks through the lobby and stops at Mr. Clyde.
Pat gives him his best, brightest smile, and an extra hearty, "Good Morning."
Old Mr. Clyde stayed grumpy.

Pat smiles anyway and walks down the street.

But a few moments later,
Pat races back, to see
Mr. Clyde squeeze out
a grumpy half smile.

Dedication

For all my family and friends who have supported me as I have chased this dream.
And for my sweet Nita...my real life Pat. - Monica Stoltzfus

To my poppa. Thank you for being one incredible dad! And thank you for all the love and support over this past year. I love you to the moon and back! Forever & Always. - Alexandra H. MacVean

Summary: Pat is a young boy living in the big city. He begins each day with a huge smile. Pat greets his fuddy-duddy doorman with this same big smile. And nothing happens-or so Pat thinks. The reader is taken on a journey following a sequence of events, unknown to the main character, unfolding just how far that simple act of a smile went. And vise versa- what may not happen when Pat decides to stay in bed all day. THE RIPPLE is inspired by the beloved It's a Wonderful Life, and aims to prove to one and all, just how important each person and a simple act of kindness can really be

Clear Fork Publishing www.clearforkpublishing.com
P.O. Box 870 102 S. Swenson Stamford, Texas 79553 (325)773-5550

Printed and Bound in the United States of America.
ISBN - 978-1-950169-21-4

CPSIA information can be obtained
at www.ICGtesting.com
Printed in the USA
LVHW070958221019
634959LV00012B/37/P